For RMR Jr.—
and
middle children,
everywhere

With many thanks to C LS and CMS

SIMON & SCHUSTER BOOKS FOR YOUNG READERS
An imprint of Simon & Schuster Children's Publishing Division
1230 Avenue of the Americas, New York, New York 10020
Copyright © 2018 by Elizabeth Rose Stanton
All rights reserved, including the right of reproduction in whole or in part in any form.
SIMON & SCHUSTER BOOKS FOR YOUNG READERS is a trademark of Simon & Schuster, Inc.
For information about special discounts for bulk purchases, please contact Simon & Schuster
Special Sales at 1-866-506-1949 or business@simonandschuster.com.
The Simon & Schuster Speakers Bureau can bring authors to your live event.
For more information or to book an event, contact the Simon & Schuster
Speakers Bureau at 1-866-248-3049 or visit our website at www.simonspeakers.com.
The text for this book was set in Reading.
The illustrations for this book were rendered in pencil and watercolor.
Manufactured in China
1017 SCP
First Edition
2 4 6 8 10 9 7 5 3 1
CIP data for this book is available from the Library of Congress.
ISBN 978-1-4814-8757-3
ISBN 978-1-4814-8758-0 (eBook)

Bub

Elizabeth Rose Stanton

A PAULA WISEMAN BOOK · SIMON & SCHUSTER BOOKS FOR YOUNG READERS

New York   London   Toronto   Sydney   New Delhi

This is Bub.

His real name is Bob.

On the first day of school
Bob didn't close
the top of his O.

Thank you,
Bub.

From then on, he was Bub.

Bub lived with his family.

Besides Maw and Paw,
the oldest was Bernice.

In the middle was Bub.

The youngest was The Baby.

She was called The Baby because

Maw and Paw could not agree on a name.

And when Maw and Paw could not agree, they could be extra LOUD.

GERTRUDE!

Giselle!

GABRIELLA!

Gladys!

This made Bub feel grumpy.

How about Bea?

And Bub felt grumpy a lot—

because he noticed a lot:

He noticed when Maw and Paw made a
fuss over Bernice and her homework,

and how they were extra,

extra quiet

whenever she picked up a bow.

And there was always *something*

going on with The Baby.

One very, very grumpy day

Bernice told Bub if he didn't be quiet, the BIG ugly monsters would come and get him.

Then she called him bubbly brain
and said it would take him
until *forever* to get his
homework done.

To make matters worse,
The Baby started calling
him Blub,

and Maw and Paw kept on
calling names, when—

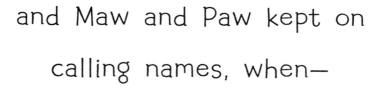

GRISELDA! Geraldine!
GINA! Gloria!

in the middle of that very,

very grumpy day—

Bub decided . . .

it was time

for a change!

For the rest of the day, things went on as usual,

until they noticed . . .

they were missing Bub!

So they left him a note:

They called out,

BUB!!

They looked

under

over

around

everywhere . . .

down

and finally . . .

UP!

They took note . . .

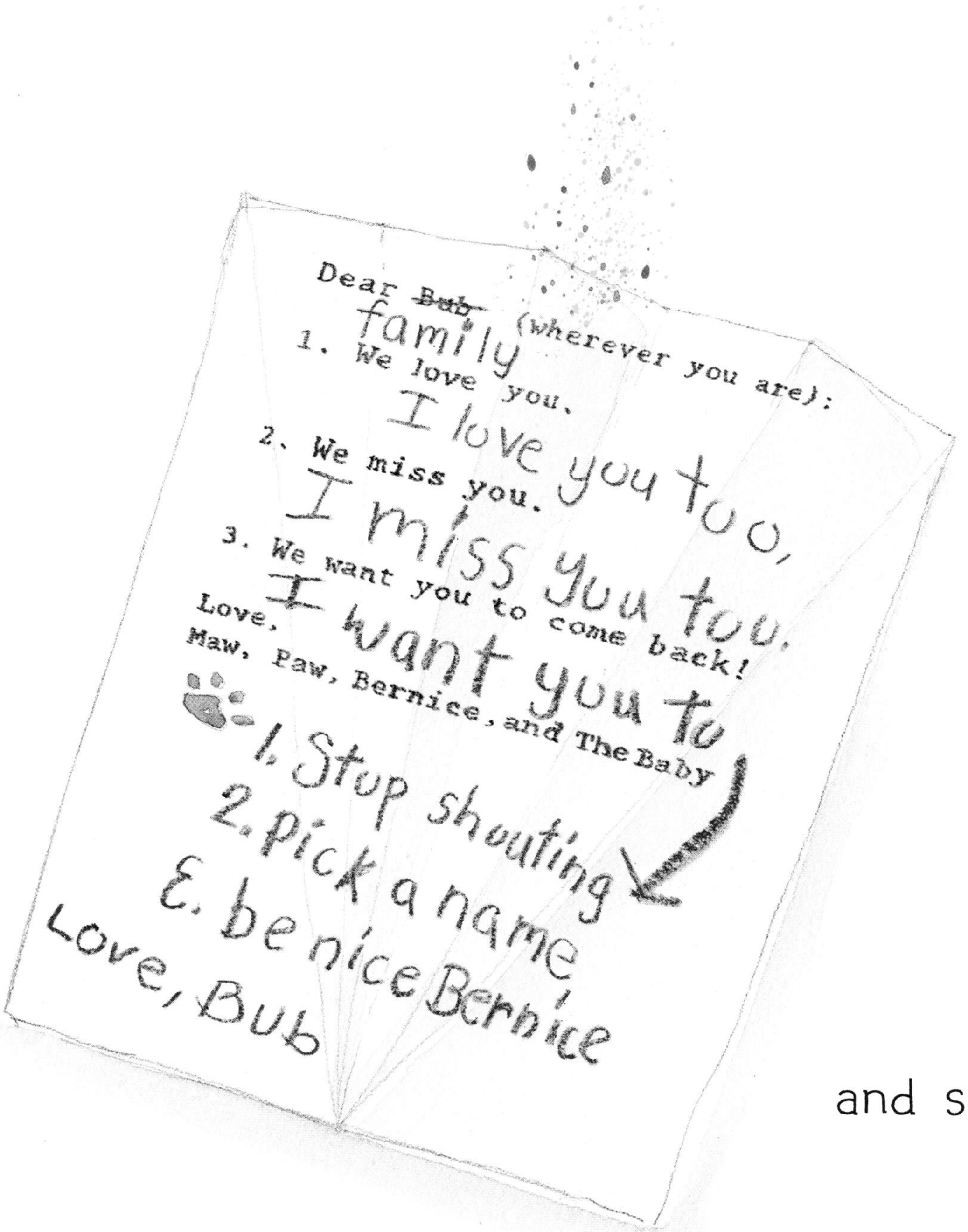

Dear ~~Bub~~ (wherever you are):

family

1. We love you.

I love you too,

2. We miss you.

I miss you too,

3. We want you to come back!

I want you to

Love,
Maw, Paw, Bernice, and The Baby

1. Stop shouting
2. pick a name
E. be nice Bernice

Love, Bub

and soon

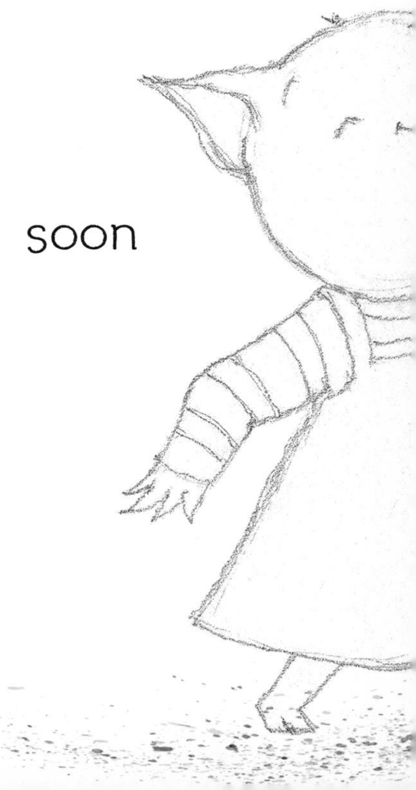

everything changed

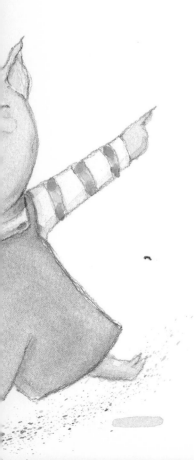

back to the way it was . . .

only better.

Impressionist Masterpieces at the Jeu de Paume, Paris

Foreword by   MICHEL LACLOTTE

Inspector-General of French Museums,
Chief Curator at the Musée du Louvre (Paintings)
and the Musée d'Orsay, Paris

Introduction by   EDWARD LUCIE-SMITH

Commentaries on the plates by   ANNE DISTEL
     CLAIRE FRÈCHES-THORY
     SYLVIE GACHE-PATIN
     GENEVIÈVE LACAMBRE

Curators at the Musée d'Orsay, Paris

With 73 color plates

THAMES AND HUDSON

Foreword and commentaries translated from the French by
Edward Lucie-Smith

Photographs supplied by the Musées nationaux, Paris

First published in the USA in 1984 by Thames and Hudson Inc.,
500 Fifth Avenue, New York, New York 10110

Library of Congress Catalog Card Number 83–50638

Color reproduction by Cliché Lux S.A., La Chaux-de-Fonds, Switzerland
Printed and bound in the Netherlands by Royal Smeets Offset b.v.

CONTENTS

Foreword   6

Introduction   8

PLATES AND COMMENTARIES   15

Frédéric Bazille   16

Eugène Boudin   18

Gustave Caillebotte   20

Mary Cassatt   22

Paul Cézanne   24

Edgar Degas   40

Paul Gauguin   56

Edouard Manet   72

Claude Monet   88

Berthe Morisot   110

Camille Pissarro   112

Pierre-Auguste Renoir   124

Alfred Sisley   136

Vincent van Gogh   146

FOREWORD

The history of the national collection of Impressionist painting, now to be seen at the Jeu de Paume museum, goes back to 1890, when Claude Monet organized a public subscription for the purchase of Manet's *Olympia* for the Musée du Luxembourg (then the official repository of modern art in Paris), fearing that otherwise it might be lost to France and go to the United States. Two years later, the state bought Renoir's *Jeunes filles au piano* from the artist. But coming as they did after years of indifference or hostility on the part of the establishment – attitudes shared by many collectors and critics – these acquisitions were not as yet real signs of official recognition. Although the Caillebotte bequest in 1895, which included masterpieces by Manet, Renoir, Cézanne, Sisley, Monet and Pissarro, was not in fact refused altogether, as legend still has it, only part of it was accepted.

The International Exhibition of 1900 marked the end of systematic opposition from the administrators of the arts, though the artists connected with the Salon and their supporters remained unreconciled to Impressionism and Post-Impressionism. Even so, a subscription organized in 1900, to acquire Gauguin's *D'où venons nous? Que sommes nous? Où allons nous? (Where Have We Come From? What Are We? Where Are We Going?)* for the Musée du Luxembourg was a failure, and the painting is now in Boston. For its formation, the national collection was forced to rely on private generosity. In 1906, Etienne Moreau-Nélaton gave, among other masterpieces, Manet's *Le déjeuner sur l'herbe*, and in 1911 Isaac de Camondo bequeathed a splendid series of works by Degas, Monet and Cézanne, as well as the collection's first Van Gogh.

Thereafter, this basic collection was augmented by a flow of acquisitions. There were gifts from the families of artists (Toulouse-Lautrec in 1902; Bazille in 1904 and 1924; Renoir in 1923; Monet in 1927; Pissarro in 1930); purchases from the Degas sale of 1917; and above all there were gifts from well-informed and generous collectors (May, Kœchlin, Pellerin, David-Weill, Rouart, Goujon, Gangnat, du Cholet, Quinn), and also from the Friends of the Musée du Luxembourg. The Personnaz bequest of 1937 was the last major acquisition before the war.

Today, we cannot but regret the fact that substantial funds for large-scale purchasing were not available in the inter-war period. They would have made it possible for France to retain a number of masterpieces from an artistic movement which, though misunderstood for so long, has now taken its proper place in history.

The light-filled Jeu de Paume museum in the Tuileries was first opened in 1947. The opening took place at a time when artists were enraptured by the idea of pure painting, and it signalled the popular triumph of Impressionism. An active purchasing policy could at long last be put in hand, and an attempt made to fill the gaps in the collection – Seurat, for example – while this was still possible. Once again collectors, and the Society of Friends of the Louvre (to which the Jeu de Paume belonged), provided effective help. There were gifts of single major works by Cézanne, Van Gogh, Gauguin and Renoir. Groups of paintings were given by important collectors such as Polignac, Charpentier, Laroche, Gourgaud, Lung, Bernheim, Halphen, Goldschmidt-Rothschild, Meyer and Kahn-Sriber, who reserved part of their collections for the Louvre. Entire collections were also donated (Gachet, 1951–54; Mollard, 1972; Kaganovitch, 1973), each reflecting not only the taste of their particular owner, but also that of an entire generation. The Jeu de Paume collection grew in another way as well, through the fact that important works of art could now be ceded in lieu of estate duties. This added some major works, among them Renoir's *La danse à la ville* and Monet's *Rue Montorgueil*, in 1978 and 1982 respectively.

Although the Jeu de Paume provided an ideal setting at the time of its opening, the building in the Tuileries is now stretched almost beyond its capacity, and it is no longer possible to exhibit the collection as it should ideally be seen, so greatly has it been enlarged over the years. (But who indeed could seriously complain about such expansion?) Nor is the building now spacious enough to cope with the ever greater numbers of visitors. Already Seurat and Toulouse-Lautrec have gone to join the other Neo-Impressionists and the Nabis in the Palais de Tokyo. In a few years, the Impressionists from the Jeu de Paume and the Post-Impressionists from the Palais de Tokyo will be reunited in a new museum now being built: the Musée d'Orsay. There they will no longer be viewed in isolation. Instead, it will be possible to compare them with work done by other artists at the same epoch. Undoubtedly, the Musée d'Orsay will provide a richer, more balanced and comprehensive view of late nineteenth-century art. Yet it is equally certain that those who have experienced the brilliance of Impressionism at the Jeu de Paume have experienced a joy which it is impossible to forget.

MICHEL LACLOTTE

INTRODUCTION

The Jeu de Paume was built as an orangery and takes its present name from the *jeu de paume*, or real tennis court, fitted up by Napoleon III in 1862 for the use of his son, the ill-fated Prince Imperial. Its role as a museum of Impressionism began as recently as 1947, and it says something for the impact made by the collections housed there that its name has become not merely world-famous but synonymous with the kind of art housed within its walls – perhaps the most popular and accessible school of art ever to have existed. More than this, the Jeu de Paume belongs to a very small group among the major museums of the world in which a particular kind of art can be experienced with an intensity available nowhere else. In this respect it resembles the Acropolis Museum in Athens, the only place where a visitor can feel the full impact of Late Archaic Greek sculpture. But unlike many other major museums – for example, its neighbour the Louvre – the Jeu de Paume's collections are not inexhaustibly enormous, and it is possible to grasp a great deal of what it has to offer on a single visit.

Impressionism marks a crisis-point in nineteenth-century art – not merely the abandonment of many ideas which had until then seemed immutably established, but the beginning of many attitudes that we still recognize as being modern and immediately relevant to ourselves. At the same time, the Impressionist movement did not spring up suddenly and in total isolation from the historical process. It is not too much to claim that French art had in one way or another been preparing for its appearance ever since the early years of the eighteenth century. Although Impressionism's immediate ancestors were the realists and naturalists of the mid-nineteenth century, its remoter ones included not only Delacroix but Watteau, Boucher, Fragonard and (gazing across the Pyrenees) a number of great Spanish masters, notably Velásquez and Goya. To insist that Impressionism is an art concerned with nothing but the immediate sensation is at best a half-truth and at worst an extremely serious error.

Yet the concern felt by the Impressionists for this immediate sensation, for the uncensored truth of the eye, conveyed without either forethought or afterthought, is something which did undoubtedly exist. When the senior painters who afterwards formed part of the group began to try to make their careers in the 1860s, during the last decade of the Second Empire, realism had already established itself as a way of seeing opposed to the conventional academic style favoured by the entrenched Salon juries. This impulse towards a less conventional way of seeing affected artists who were themselves deeply conservative by temperament. We meet with interesting examples in the early work of Degas, for instance in his painting of *La famille Bellelli*, which dates from 1858–60. Here there is a new attitude to composition, evidently inspired by photography – one of the many scientific inventions of the period. These inventions, added together, were completely to alter man's perception of the world, and the Impressionists were the first artists to make a fundamental response to the change.

When Daguerre announced the perfection of his invention in 1839, enthusiasm for it spread like wildfire, because the nineteenth-century bourgeois public had already anticipated, and with some impatience, a democratization of the whole image-making process. What fascinated early enthusiasts for photography was not merely the notion that nature could now be persuaded to make her own portrait (the camera lens was deemed to be an entirely objective means of recording reality), but that photographic plates captured that reality with a fidelity and a regard for detail hitherto unattainable. The one thing that early photographs lacked, and it was a major omission, was colour.

The nature of colour, and the way in which the human eye perceived it, had naturally enough also attracted the scientific curiosity of the nineteenth century, and the Impressionist masters were the first artists to put the scientists' discoveries into effect. The conclusion of the theorists was that the whole gamut of colours derived in fact from a few pure tones, which blended optically on the retina. It became the ambition of the Impressionist group to demonstrate the truth of this contention by painting in small, pure touches that coalesced to create the required hue only when the spectator stood at a certain distance from the canvas. And in order to achieve a perfect reproduction of what the eye really perceived, the Impressionists believed that pictures were, as far as possible, to be created in the open air, in the very presence of what the artist was depicting.

If this had been all there was to it, the Impressionists would have remained purely a school of landscape painters. And indeed, as the visitor to the Jeu de Paume will see, landscape subjects do loom very large in their total output. Certain members of the group, notably Alfred Sisley, produced virtually nothing else. It may be unconventional to begin a survey of Impressionist aims with Sisley instead of with greater and more all-encompassing masters such as Manet and Monet, but there is real reason for doing so. Sisley's beautiful *L'inondation à Port-Marly*, painted in 1876, and one of the very finest of all his pictures, shows the close link between Impressionism and somewhat earlier practitioners of *plein air* landscape painting such as Corot. The treatment of the house on the left is very much in Corot's manner, even though the floodwaters themselves are treated with a much broader and more glittering touch. A picture done two years earlier, Sisley's *Le brouillard* of 1874, because of the very nature of its subject, gives a notion of the extremes to which the Impressionists could take their particular view of landscape. The painting seems at first sight to be almost without structure, a capricious piling up of variously coloured dots. What one has here is not a painting of a particular spot, but an attempt to capture a particular effect of light. The locality of the painting is irrelevant. So is the idea of trying to convey intellectual content as opposed to physical sensation.

This line of thinking was to be carried to extremes by Claude Monet in the latter part of his career. One of Monet's innovations was to paint the same motif over and over again. There are long series devoted to the west façade of Rouen Cathedral (two examples are illustrated in this book), to a group of haystacks in a field, and to the waterlilies which filled the ponds in the garden Monet created for himself at Giverny. The Jeu de Paume, which previously lacked one of these late paintings of waterlilies, has recently been fortunate enough to fill the gap with a splendid example.

Monet may have chosen Rouen Cathedral as the subject for one of these series with polemical intent, since here was a major Gothic structure infused with a wide range of meanings for all Frenchmen, and indeed for all Europeans who might see it. But these meanings were something the painter simply chose to ignore. He was intent only on recording the permutations of light and atmosphere on the complex façade, whose sole function was to modulate the atmospheric flux and make it visible. The Impressionist obsession with analysis of light and the process of seeing becomes the be-all and end-all of art; everything else is pushed aside as an irrelevance. And this of course implies a view of the world and of the painter's role in it that would have seemed not only outrageous but actually incomprehensible when Monet first began to paint, at Le Havre under Boudin's tuition, towards the end of the 1850s.

Monet's studies of *La cathédrale de Rouen* are of especial importance because they are the clearest demonstration of the way in which Impressionism altered the morality of painting. Until the middle of the nineteenth century, it had been a universally agreed idea that art was meant to express some moral standpoint espoused by the artist. This notion informs even the work of Gustave Courbet, the great mid-century realist who preceded the Impressionists and who had occasioned so much controversy among French art critics and the public. Impressionism changed all this. It declared morals in paintings to be irrelevant, yet at the same time it turned the actual practice of painting into a series of moral choices: the painter had to be completely true to his own feelings concerning the nature of art. It is this conviction which links two artists otherwise as different from one another as Monet and Cézanne.

The question of morality and the painter's attitude to it is also extremely relevant in the case of Manet, who otherwise seems to fit rather uneasily into the Impressionist group. The Jeu de Paume is fortunate enough to possess, amongst a superlative group of paintings by this artist, two works which were amongst the most controversial of their whole epoch: *Le déjeuner sur l'herbe* and *Olympia*, both painted in 1863. *Le déjeuner sur l'herbe* was described by an outraged contemporary critic as follows: 'A commonplace woman of the demi-monde, as naked as can be, shamelessly lolls between two dandies dressed to the teeth.' He went on to call the painting 'a young man's practical joke, a shameful open sore not worth exhibiting in this way.' The irony was that Manet had made use of the most approved classic sources – the composition derives directly from a Renaissance engraving by Marcantonio Raimondi, after Raphael, and is strongly reminiscent of Titian's *Concert champêtre*, then as now one of the glories of the Louvre. *Olympia*, a reclining nude indebted both to Goya's *Naked Maja* and Titian's *Venus of Urbino*, aroused an equivalent anger among conservative critics, who translated into social and moral terms their disapproval of Manet's technical radicalism – his reduction of gradations of tone, and his emphasis on outline and on the importance of the picture-plane. Manet was not at this stage experimenting with optical mixtures, though he painted magnificent *plein air* scenes in the course of his career – *Sur la plage*, of 1873, is a particularly beautiful example.

Sur la plage is also an example of something else: the Impressionists' ability to render the very texture of life in their time. This, even more than their brilliant freshness of colour, is the quality that has made them so firmly beloved by the public. A number of extremely familiar examples of this gift can be found in these pages – Manet's own *La serveuse de bocks*, Renoir's incomparable *Moulin de la Galette*, and most of all a whole series of paintings and pastels by Degas. Indeed, Degas was perhaps, among all the contributors to the various Impressionist exhibitions, the one most determined to reflect what he saw as the nature of contemporary life. Yet of all the major Impressionists he remains, I think, the one who is most often misunderstood by the public.

What attitude are we meant to take, for example, towards one of the best-known of all his versions of contemporary urban life, the *Au café* of 1876? Its alternative title, *L'absinthe*, suggests that this may be an exception among Impressionist pictures in having a directly moral purpose, and it is certainly one where any trace of *joie de vivre* seems to be absent – two melancholic figures seated side by side, their psychological distance from one another stressed by their physical proximity. Degas seems to imply a comment on the meaningless character of daily life. But the comment, if there is one, is made with sophisticated obliqueness. Degas is fascinated by the world of Parisian entertainment, but he sees it characteristically in terms of work – the players in *L'orchestre de l'Opéra* are men doing a job, oblivious to events on the stage. The members of *La classe de danse* are similarly preoccupied with what is for them labour, though for others it will become entertainment.

The Impressionists were not united in their political views. Degas' opinions were conservative, whereas Camille Pissarro was a Socialist, but their work is surprisingly eloquent about their commitment to the world as they found it. The delightful high-jinks of the Moulin de la Galette can be put against the background supplied not only by Degas' weary *Les repasseuses* but also against the smoke and grime of Monet's *La gare Saint-Lazare* and the frankly industrial quality of Pissarro's view of *Le port de Rouen, Saint-Sever*. All these works express the conviction that painting must come out of ordinary life, and continue to march in step with it.

Pissarro is perhaps the most difficult to characterize of all the Impressionists, and there are some signs, particularly his venture into a more systematic kind of Neo-Impressionism under the influence of Seurat (see, for instance, his *Femme dans un clos ... Eragny*), which indicate that he found it difficult to characterize himself. It is, in fact, in Pissarro's œuvre that we sometimes glimpse some of the losses as well as the gains in Impressionism's determination to eschew any kind of moral message. Pissarro's noble, thoughtful *Self-portrait* of 1873 gives us more than a glimpse of a nature which all his colleagues respected for its generosity and gentleness. And the charming *Jeune fille à la baguette* shows Pissarro's secret hankering for a kind of art which Impressionist doctrine seemed to make impossible – the profoundly touching peasant scenes of J. F. Millet. But Pissarro himself is never able to achieve the kind of resonance which Millet reaches. To be sure, his finest landscapes, like the *Entrée du village de Voisins*, are marvellously executed but still leave us with the feeling that there is something missing, some essential element of himself which the artist has been unable to express – though perhaps this is simply the hindsight that comes from knowing a certain amount about Pissarro's life.

It is interesting to remember, at any rate, that Millet was also a primary source for Vincent van Gogh, who is one of the three major Post-Impressionist painters (along with Cézanne and Gauguin) whose work is also exhibited at the Jeu de Paume. Van Gogh, however, is not perhaps the one with whom one would choose to start, if one wants to understand how Impressionist attitudes eventually came to seem constricting. The master one must turn to is Cézanne.

Cézanne spent a period of his career as an Impressionist painter in a strictly technical sense – he even showed in the Impressionist exhibitions of 1874 and 1877, which made him an official member of the group. At this stage he was chiefly influenced by Pissarro, whom he had known as early as 1862, when he worked at the Académie Suisse. The curious satirical work *Une moderne Olympia*, showing the squat balding artist goggling at the naked goddess uncovered for his inspection, may express some of the doubts that long plagued him. Cézanne only fully discovered his own method and his own potentialities in 1882, when he went to live at Aix-en-Provence. It was then that he seemingly abandoned Impressionist precepts in favour of their complete opposite. But in fact this abandonment is already becoming apparent in *La maison du pendu*, painted as early as 1873. And it is of course entirely visible in later work such as *Le vase bleu* and *Nature morte aux oignons*. These latter paintings are both classical examples of Cézanne's preoccupation with absolutely commonplace subject-matter, which he uses as the raw material for a stringent, immutable pictorial architecture having nothing to do with the impression made by the fleeting moment or a particular effect of light. Writing to Emile Bernard in 1904, Cézanne said:

The writer expresses himself by means of abstractions, whereas the painter concretises his sensations and perceptions in line and colour. One is not over-scrupulous, nor over-sincere, nor over-submissive to nature, but one has more or less mastered one's model, and above all one's means of expression. One must enter into the object one is observing and strive to express it in the most logical manner possible.

The full consequences of pursuing this doctrine to its logical conclusion can be seen in the great canvases of *Baigneurs*, painted between 1890 and 1900, and especially in the more drastic of two versions of this subject in the Jeu de Paume collection. Here one notes how the ostensible subject matter has become a mere pretext for the act of making a painting, which Cézanne sees in terms of a surface completely organized by means of colour and line, a statement sufficient to itself, without reference to anything outside.

If Cézanne depersonalizes art, the opposite is true of the work of Gauguin and Van Gogh. There are few artists where our knowledge of the biographical facts matters so much to our appreciation of what they do. Van Gogh did not encounter Impressionism first-hand until 1886, when he came to Paris to join his brother Theo, and his canvases touched by its influence do not reveal the full extent of his powers. In fact, if Impressionism based itself on the objective evaluation of appearance, and in particular of the effects of light, Van Gogh pursued an almost opposite line. His method was to project his own emotions on to what he saw. The famous canvas showing *La chambre de Van Gogh à Arles* is not simply a representation of a commonplace room but is instead a reflection of a highly charged state of feeling, symbolized both by the objects the room contains and by the way these objects, and indeed the very space they occupy, are depicted. The same is true of the later painting of *L'église d'Auvers-sur-Oise*, which was done in 1890, the year of Van Gogh's suicide, and which radiates the manic intensity of the artist's state of mind. One has only to imagine what Sisley or Pissarro might have made of the same subject to see how totally different Van Gogh's intentions are. His portraits, and especially his self-portraits, are similarly subjective, a search not so much for truth to physical appearances as for the spirit which lives within a man.

Van Gogh did not set out to found a school: Gauguin did. There was always in him something of the teacher and leader, and he adopted Impressionism (like Cézanne, he was introduced to it by Pissarro) only in order to reject it. Gauguin's real independence of Impressionism began with his first visit to Pont-Aven in Brittany in 1886, though the final break did not come until the following year, as a result of his contact with the young Emile Bernard, who was busy preaching the superiority of synthesis – the bringing together of all elements of an experience, subjective as well as objective – to the mere analysis of appearances, which is what Impressionism was all about.

The final stage of Gauguin's rejection of everything Impressionism stood for is marked by his departure for Tahiti in 1891, in search of a completely different world. The pictures he painted during his two residences in the South Seas – he returned to France in 1893 only to set out again in 1895 – are those which have fixed his image forever in the popular mind. Even though we know that Gauguin was guilty of fictionalizing what he found, the act of creating these Tahitian paintings, even in defiance of the facts, answered a pressing need within himself, and that was the point of producing them. The voyage to the South Seas was not as decisive as has been claimed. It is, for example, interesting to compare Gauguin's images of *luxe, calme et volupté* with certain late paintings by Renoir, most of all perhaps with the wonderful double nude *Les baigneuses*, which Renoir painted in 1918–19 at the very end of a long creative life. No more than Gauguin's South Sea beauties do these have anything to do with what the artist has actually observed. The pretence that appearances are being meticulously analysed (never very strong in Renoir's work) has long since been abandoned. What we get instead is a sensual hymn of praise for the richness offered by the life of the senses.

I suggested towards the beginning of this essay that the roots of Impressionism are at least partly to be found in the French eighteenth century. Renoir has a strong neo-rococo streak, itself very much in keeping with certain aspects of French late-nineteenth-century taste, and *Les baigneuses* certainly serves to reinforce the comparison – with nudes by Boucher, for example. But it also suggests a more general idea. The durable appeal of the Impressionists is not to be found simply in the sparkle of the typical Impressionist palette. It has also something to do with a fundamental rationality of attitude, a willingness to accept the nature of the world and to express a frank delight in its sensual surface. The *homme moyen sensuel* in most of us will return gratefully to a school which proved that it is one of the functions of art to make us see more intensely and perfectly what everyone is capable of perceiving. No painters ever fulfilled this function better than the Impressionist masters.

Edward Lucie-Smith

PLATES AND COMMENTARIES

The following abbreviations have been used for the authors' names:

AD   Anne Distel

CF-T Claire Frèches-Thory

SG-P Sylvie Gache-Patin

GL   Geneviève Lacambre

Frédéric BAZILLE (1841–1870)

L'atelier de Bazille (*Bazille's Studio*), 1869–70

Oil on canvas, 38⅝ × 50⅝ (98 × 128.5)

Bequest of Marc Bazille, brother of the artist, 1924 (R.F. 2449)

Bazille, who came from a well-known family in Montpellier, was a friend of Bruyas, Courbet's patron. He arrived in Paris in 1862 and that autumn entered Gleyre's studio, where he became friendly with Monet, Renoir and Sisley. In the spring of 1863, these young artists, their enthusiasm fired by Manet's paintings shown at the Galerie Martinet and later by those at the Salon des Refusés (see p. 74), elected him as their leader. It is this group of friends which Bazille depicts here, at his studio in the Batignolles quarter of Paris, which he occupied from 1 January 1868 to 15 May 1870.

Once he had returned from the summer holidays of 1869, and had had black curtains put up which allowed him to paint without interruption, Bazille started work on several paintings. They included a studio interior and a female nude for the Salon – pictures which were to occupy him all winter. The female nude *La toilette* (*The Toilet*) (Musée de Montpellier) is depicted unfinished in this work, hanging above the sofa. It was rejected by the Salon of 1870. Also visible to the left is the *Pêcheur à l'epervier* (*Fisherman with a Net*), rejected in 1869. Behind the easel is the *Tireuse de cartes* (*The Fortune-teller*), while the large painting on the wall above the piano is *Terrasse de Méric* (*The Terrace at Méric*) of 1867 (Musée de Montpellier). Above the pianist (Edmond Maître, a friend of Bazille), a still-life by Monet is a reminder that Bazille helped the artist by buying his work, notably *Femmes au jardin* (see p. 88). On the easel is the *Vue de village* (*View of a Village*) of 1868 (Musée de Montpellier), which Manet is examining, hat on head. The artist had a profound influence on Bazille, as he himself acknowledged when he wrote to his father on 1 January 1870: 'Manet has made me what I am.' Bazille is the tall slim figure in the centre of the picture. The identification of the three figures to the left is less certain. It depends on two contradictory statements made by Monet, probably after the Bazille retrospective at the Salon d'Automne of 1910, where this picture was exhibited. Are we to identify the man next to Manet as Monet or Zacharie Astruc? And are those grouped to the left Renoir and Zola, or Monet and Sisley? These artists and writers were among Manet's admirers, and were depicted by Fantin-Latour at the same epoch in his *L'atelier des Batignolles* (*Studio at Batignolles*, Jeu de Paume). But, unlike Fantin-Latour, who remained faithful to the example of the Dutch masters, Bazille has produced a totally modern composition, which evokes the quasi-bourgeois atmosphere of the place where he liked to entertain his friends. His death in battle a few months later makes this work, painted for his own pleasure, a particularly moving testament.   GL

Eugène BOUDIN (1824–1898)

La plage de Trouville (*The Beach at Trouville*), 1864

Oil on panel, $10\frac{1}{4} \times 18\frac{1}{8}$ (26×48)

Gift of Eduardo Mollard, 1961 (R.F. 1961–26)

Boudin's début in the domain of art was a modest one, beginning as he did as a paper-merchant and framer at Le Havre, and using his shop to show work by painters such as Troyon and Millet who passed through the town. These men encouraged him to paint, and a grant from the town council enabled him to go and study in Paris in 1851. But he always remained faithful to the Normandy coast, where in 1858 he met Claude Monet, whose first teacher he became. He also got to know Courbet and Baudelaire; the latter was delighted with his sky studies, and supported him when he exhibited at the Salon for the first time in 1859 with an ambitious and relatively large work, *Le pardon de Sainte-Anne-la-Palud* (*The Pardon of Sainte-Anne-la-Palud*, now in the museum at Le Havre). The painting depicts a picturesque throng gathered round white tents and market-stalls exposed to the open air, all set in a wide blue landscape.

Certain elements from *Le pardon de Sainte-Anne-la-Palud* – among them the hill and the chapel with its bell-tower – occur again here in this delightful little painting of the beach at Trouville. To the right are the high slate roofs of a villa, and the hill behind the beach; in the centre are summer visitors, standing about, or seated on chairs, with brilliant white bathing cabins and two tall flag-poles in the background. All of this occupies only the bottom of a composition in which the sky occupies most of the space.

In the same year that this was painted, Boudin met Courbet and Manet at Trouville, which was then a smart watering-place. He had started to paint its bustling fashionable society in 1862, on the advice of Eugène Isabey, a member of the Barbizon School. In 1863 he depicted *L'impératrice Eugénie et sa suite à Trouville* (*The Empress Eugenie and Her Suite at Trouville*, Glasgow Museums and Art Galleries, Burrell Collection) in a dazzling swirl of crinolines, and submitted *La plage de Trouville* to the Salon in 1864.

Out of loyalty to his Impressionist friends, Boudin took part in the first Impressionist exhibition of 1874, but thereafter remained faithful to the Salon, which did not hold his temporary apostasy against him.   GL

Gustave CAILLEBOTTE (1848–1894)

Voiliers à Argenteuil (*Sailing-boats at Argenteuil*), c. 1888

Oil on canvas, $25\frac{5}{8} \times 21\frac{5}{8}$ (65×55)

Purchased in 1954 (R.F. 1954–31)

Caillebotte came from an upper-middle-class family and inherited a substantial fortune on the death of his father in 1873, which allowed him to pursue his vocation as an artist. Having been a pupil of Bonnat, he entered the Ecole des Beaux-Arts in 1873, but left it early after his work was rejected by the Salon in 1875. It was probably through Degas, who was a friend of Bonnat, that he came into contact with the Impressionist group, then newly established. From 1876 onwards he participated in its exhibitions, playing an important part as organizer, but twice did not exhibit (in 1881 and 1886) after dissensions within the group.

His early work is characterized by a daring naturalism, taking urban life as its theme, but he returned deliberately to Impressionist methods in his brilliant Argenteuil period. He thus seemed old-fashioned, or at any rate lagging behind the times, when he exhibited his work in 1888 at Durand-Ruel's gallery, and with the Group of XX in Brussels where he showed paintings of boats on the Seine. Some, such as the one reproduced here, are expecially successful in the balance of their composition and evocation of the quality of light. Since 1882 Caillebotte had owned a house by the river, with a large flower-filled garden, at Le Petit-Gennevilliers, across the river from Argenteuil. He settled here permanently in 1887. The river bank and the landing-stage near his house appear in this picture, and on the horizon, behind the old wooden bridge at Argenteuil, are the supports of the railway bridge and the hills of Sanois and Orgemont.

Caillebotte is equally famous for the role he played as patron of his friends the Impressionists as he is as a painter – in fact in 1876 he made them beneficiaries of his first will. Thanks to him, many of their paintings entered the Musée du Luxembourg (then the museum of modern art in Paris) in 1896, despite both the refusal of part of his legacy and the scandal which followed the opening of the Caillebotte room in 1897. He was also one of those who subscribed to buy Manet's *Olympia* – the first work by this artist to enter the French national collections (see p. 76). GL

G. Caillebotte

Mary CASSATT (1844–1926)

Femme cousant (*Woman Sewing*), *c.* 1880–82

Oil on canvas, 36¼ × 24¾ (92 × 63)

Antonin Personnaz bequest, 1937 (R.F. 1937–20)

Like Eva Gonzalès and Berthe Morisot, who were pupils of Manet, Mary Cassatt was one of the special and unusual women connected with the Impressionist movement. Daughter of a rich Pittsburgh banker, she wanted to be a painter from a very early age. To achieve her ambition, she had to brave the scepticism and mockery of her family, at a time when it was not at all the thing for a woman to be an artist. Disappointed by the quality of the art instruction available in the United States, she soon returned to France where she had already spent part of her early childhood. After a short period in the studio of the Salon painter Chaplin, a good technician who specialized in society portraits, she turned resolutely to the study of the Old Masters, copying them with great enthusiasm during her travels in Italy, Spain, Belgium and Holland. She also tried her luck at the Paris Salon, where in 1874 Degas took special note of one of the portraits she had submitted: 'There is someone who thinks like me', he said to Joseph Tourny, a mutual friend.

Degas, for whom Cassatt had the greatest admiration, nevertheless waited three years before coming to visit her studio and inviting her to take part in the fourth Impressionist exhibition of 1879 – which she did, with *La loge* (*The Theatre Box*) and *La tasse de thé* (*The Cup of Tea*). She also showed in the fifth (1880), sixth (1881), and last Impressionist exhibitions (1886). One of the works she showed was the *Femme cousant*, reproduced here, which then became part of the famous collection left to the Louvre by Antonin Personnaz.

Though several of Cassatt's paintings are close to Manet (*Jeune femme en noir* [*Young Woman in Black*], 1833) and to Renoir (*A l'Opéra* [*At the Opera*], 1880), her work as a whole shows that she never swerved from her admiration for Japanese art. This is evident above all in the important series of prints which Cassatt showed so proudly at her first solo exhibition, held at Durand-Ruel's gallery in 1891. Moreover, she confines herself almost entirely to images of women and children, and achieves powerful effects within an intimist framework, as evinced by *Femme cousant*, which also demonstrates her exceptional talent as a colourist. It should not be forgotten that, by encouraging Durand-Ruel to show the Impressionists in the United States, and by becoming the enlightened adviser of the great American collector H. O. Havemeyer, Cassatt played a major role in the diffusion of Impressionism on the other side of the Atlantic. CF-T